The
Seduction
of the
Senses

The
Seduction
of the
Senses

A publication of
Fashioned In His Image, Inc.

Cover Design by Fatima Frost

*Unless otherwise indicated, all Scripture quotations are taken
from the King James Version of the Holy Bible.*

© Copyright 2003 – Fashioned In His Image, Inc.

Library of Congress Control Number: 2003103974

Serenity Publishing and Communications
P.O Box 282282
Nashville, TN 37228

FASHIONED IN HIS IMAGE, INC.
340-A W. Trinity Lane
Suite 108
Nashville, TN 37207

ISBN 0-9712701-4-7

Dedication

We dedicate this book
to all of the women of
Fashioned In His Image, Inc.
whose courage and character
in spite of experiences
have inspired us to new depths of
understanding the riches of God's grace.

Acknowledgments

We would like to express our gratitude to several people whose assistance and support have been invaluable in the writing of this book:
Pastor Horace E. Hockett, for his prayers and unflagging faith in what the Father God had called us to do and staunch encouragement that we could do it;

Sister Kiwanis Hockett, who received the mandate from God, provided the initial impetus and was the driving force behind our collaboration;

Dr. Kathleen Kilcrease (Aunt Kat), whose insight and considerable talent is currently going into producing a study guide to accompany this book;

Dr. Karen Brown-Dunlap, whose fervent belief in the importance of this work and diligent efforts in editing it were immensely helpful;

And to our Born Again Church family~whose intercession, faith and encouragement is always a source of blessing.

Foreword

The road to Kissimmee, Florida, glistens with promise. Usually it is the promise of a visit to Disney World: a promise of quick fun and fantasy. For me, the promise was of a reunion with my sisters from Nashville's Born Again Church, a time of fellowship and faith.

Ahead, in a spacious suburban home, seven ladies labored with a special goal: they would produce a book that captured Spirit-filled messages from the Fashioned in His Image (Born Again's women's ministry) annual women's conferences.

I thought about life's strange paths as I drove on the roads to Kissimmee. A day earlier I had been in New York, convened with other journalists judging the Pulitzer Prizes. On my return home to Tampa, I got a voice mail telling me that friends from my former church home were gathered in Kissimmee and wanted me to join them as they produced a book. On this morning instead of driving west to work, I found myself headed east to see old friends. I thought about our lives, the trials and successes, the love and lasting sisterhood. My mind drifted to the words of a song on my stereo: "Like the dew in the morning, (Let the word of the Spirit) gently rest upon my heart."

When I arrived at the house I found a combination of Bible-study, slumber party and ordered platoon on a mission. Ladies wrote and edited on computers and printers deployed around the house. Others researched Biblical information, debated points for clarification, cooked or organized. All responded to the cheerful insistence of Sister Kitty Hockett, associate minister with her husband, Pastor Horace Hockett, of Born Again. Spirit-filled music soothed the work, and a sister told me they had paused on one song during their morning devotion. The words said, "May He (the Holy Spirit) gently rest upon my heart."

Steadily, the book came together. It tells of the life God intended for us, a life of order, peace and fulfillment, and of how we depart from the plan through disobedience, ignorance, and self-delusion. It also tells of God's plan for restoring us, of bringing us out of the world's chaos and into His peace. This book's message is told through the lives of men and women in the Bible, and it's told by sisters, fashioned in His image, who have each faced struggles and who turn to God's Word for daily living.

In many ways this book mirrors the road to Kissimmee. In life we can choose the path of a day's fun and fantasy. We can kid ourselves, enjoy the thrills of a day, and suffer the long nights of consequences. Or we can choose a different path, a road of fellowship with Christ, of living faith, and lasting joy.

Come journey with us. Maybe this book will be a reminder of God's will for your life. Maybe it will clarify the messages you've heard for years. Or maybe this will be the first time you've ever heard God's plan for personal peace. Wherever you are, come join us. May this book bless you. May you choose your paths wisely. And may the word of the Spirit, gently rest upon your heart.

Dr. Karen Brown Dunlap
Dean/President-designate
Poynter Institute
St. Petersburg, FL

Contents

Introduction

Another child dies from abuse.
Another marriage ends in divorce.
Another day of depression and lost purpose.
Another dream dies.
We accept it as the way life has to be; yet, that
was never God's plan.

Many of the destructive behaviors that plague our society, our families, and our lives are inherited from generation to generation and many are learned. Destructive behaviors have taken priority over our values and our integrity, and have become a way of life for millions today. These habits, which stem from our rejection or ignorance of God's original design for mankind, affect our well being and the well being of those around us, even generations to come. God's plan for mankind, however, offers life more abundantly. The Word of God offers solutions to any problem.

THE SEDUCTION OF THE SENSES will bring an awareness of how destructive habits have caused us to live beneath our privilege and even caused death. The godly principles offered will renew your mind, break bondages, and bring you into greater understanding and into a new relationship with God.

Before going to the next page, ask the Father God to open your heart and mind that you may receive deliverance, healing, restoration, and understanding of God's original plan for man in these God-given principles.

God's Original
Design for Man

CHAPTER 1

God's Original Design for Man

He was born into great promise and opportunity. He thought things would always be that way. However, life crumbled for this child of privilege when he was five years old.

His father was killed, his home destroyed and he was crippled for life in an accident. Taken in by family acquaintances, he looked ahead to life in the worst part of town. He was entitled to a rich inheritance, but that all slipped away.

What do you do when life falls apart, or when things just seem confusing and meaningless? What is the hope for each day? How do you find purpose for the future?

Consider the biblical story of the life of Mephibosheth (Me-fib-o-sheth) told in 2 Samuel 9. He was the grandson of King Saul and the son of Jonathan. When Mephibosheth was five years old his grandfather and father were killed in battle. Fearing for the child's life, his nurse fled with Mephibosheth. In her haste, she stumbled and dropped him, leaving him maimed for life. He was carried to a house at Lo-debar, a hideous place.

The name means desolate or dark alley.

His life started in tragedy; he lived in gloom but God had better things ahead for Mephibosheth. This brief story of a young man who experienced both great despair and great blessing in his lifetime, holds rich lessons about God's plan for our lives, the choices we make to be led by our senses or something higher, about loss and recovery, generational curses or blessings, and right relationships.

When God created man, His plan was to bring forth many sons and daughters who would be a reflection of His image and glory, with whom He could commune in intimate fellowship.

> *Then God said, "Let us make man in our image, according to Our likeness..." So God created man in His own image; in the image of God He created him; Male and female He created them.*
> *Genesis 1:26, 27 (NKJV)*

Throughout the Bible, we are shown that man is the supreme object of God's love, and in return, he was created to love and worship God, and to live in eternal fellowship with his Creator.

All the earth shall worship you and sing praises to You. They shall sing praises to your name.

Psalm 66:4 (NKJV)

The Bible tells us that God is Spirit. It is a mystery, but 1 John 5:7 tells us that God exists in three parts, a triune state: God the Father, God the Son (the Word, Jesus Christ), and God the Holy Spirit. Ideally, our fellowship with God was intended to mirror the unity, agreement, harmony, love and purpose displayed in the relationship of the Father, Son, and Holy Spirit (*the Godhead*).

Just as the Godhead has three parts, the Creator made man a three-part being: spirit, soul and body (1 Thessalonians 5:23, Hebrews 4:12.) Just as the Godhead is one in unity to carry out God's will and purpose, so God's intention is for man's three parts to work together to carry out His will and purpose in the earth. As man comes in line with God's plan, he can live a life that is whole, healthy, blessed, prosperous, productive and joyful, regardless of circumstances.

How could life have been any of these things for Mephibosheth? The Bible doesn't tell much about his thoughts, but it does say that later in life he described himself as a "dead dog." Not just a dog, but a dead dog. There were few things lower in the Hebrew culture than a dead dog.

Why did Mephibosheth feel this way? Maybe it was because he was led by what he could see, feel and think about. He saw himself as the crippled member of a deposed dynasty. He felt the pain and scorn of his physical handicap. He probably thought of himself as homeless, inferior and fearful, while living in a dangerous dump.

How could he have come in line with God's will for his life? How could he maintain an attitude of hope instead of succumbing to bitterness? Even as he lived in defeat, God was moving on his behalf. Victory would come for Mephibosheth when he shifted his focus from the natural to the spiritual, from things of the world to the will of God. But, he would have to be willing to reach out and embrace God's plan.

Think of how the world can overwhelm our spirits. Our usual means of interacting with the physical world is through our body, directed by our mind and emotions (our soul). Our means of interacting and communing with God and being led and directed by Him, however, is through our spirit. Our soul was intended to be the medium for processing and maintaining the information gathered from our interaction with the world, including our interaction with others. Our soul's responses, which are carried out through our body, were always intended by God to be directed and guided by His Spirit, living within our spirit.

In the beginning, man's fellowship with God was perfect, complete, and harmonious. Adam walked with God in the cool of the day, managed the Garden of Eden, exercised dominion in the earth and lived in peaceful bliss with his wife, Eve. Adam was in the image of God — his spirit, soul and body were perfectly coordinated and integrated, functioning together as God designed. He enjoyed unbroken communion with God, his Creator, and was in intimate relationship with Him—hearing His voice, sensing His presence, obeying His will. This was Adam's natural lifestyle. He was whole, healthy, productive and blessed.

However, when Adam and Eve sinned, all of this— God's original plan for how man was to live and operate in the earth—was suddenly turned upside down. No longer did God govern us, but instead, our spirits became darkened without the life and light of His Spirit. Man became spiritually dead. (Genesis 2:17, 3:17, Ephesians 2:5, Colossians 2:13)

Separated from God, cut off from the fellowship and communion that we were created for, and without the guidance and direction of His Spirit, man veered further off track, and that has led to untold sorrow, hardship, heartbreak, self-indulgence, and misery. Man became a slave to his own fallen nature, self-will, and corrupted thoughts and desires.

Instead of reflecting God's image and likeness, we find man imaging a very different reality, one that has its origin in Satan's deception and therefore suffering the consequences of every kind of destructive behavior imaginable. This partnering with death spawns addictions, depression, uncontrollable anger, unforgiveness, low self-esteem, greed, selfishness, pride, lust, fear, unnatural affections, co-dependency, insecurity, paranoia, and the list goes on, causing man to lose the abundance of life's treasures God intended for him to enjoy.

Thanks be to God, who sent His Son, Jesus Christ, to redeem us back to Himself. We can return to God's original plan for our lives and be restored to the spiritual, emotional, mental, and physical health and wholeness He intended for us to enjoy from the very beginning. We can be restored to the fellowship and communion with God for which we were created.

How do we get started on this journey to wholeness? How can we break out of the bondage that sin and separation from God and its devastating consequences have produced in our lives? The first step is to receive the salvation that Christ offers, then we must get back to basics. We must get a clear understanding of our God-given nature and how it was designed to function. With this understanding, we can begin to be restored to God's original plan.

As we noted, man is a triune being; we exist on three dimensions. We are spirit, soul, and body. Let's explore each dimension.

SPIRIT

The spirit is the part of you that is GOD-conscious. The spirit of man is the highest part of our three-fold nature. It is the part in which God dwells by His Spirit if we are born again. That is, if we've accepted Jesus Christ as our Savior. It is also the part of man that enables us to connect and communicate with God, and the vehicle through which God communicates directly and intimately with us. It is the part that God uses to direct us and reveal truth to us. Proverbs 20:27: *"The spirit of man is the candle of the Lord..."*

Because of sin, man's spirit is dead to God and must be born again. Without this regeneration, man doesn't have God's guidance and is lost in sin. But when we are born again, God's Spirit comes to dwell in our spirit and we are made alive to God once again. We are able to commune with Him and to receive instruction. Most important of all, we receive eternal life. The spirit is where man's conscience, the ability to "know right from wrong" independent of our intellect or senses, resides.

SOUL

The soul is the part of you that is SELF-conscious.The soul of man is the seat of our personality and self-life. It is a highly influential part of our nature and is the determining agent of our actions through our mind, emotions and will. It includes our intellect, (thinking and reasoning) sensibilities and feelings, and our power to choose and to act.

The feelings include the emotions, affections, desires, and sentiments. The emotions are basically personal feelings, in other words, they are involved with self, and include both pleasant and painful feelings such as joy, pride, hope, peace, sorrow, shame, despair, and fear.

The affections are more complex than emotions. They involve feelings toward others and go beyond self to an object. The affections can be positive or negative feelings: love, compassion, sympathy, gratitude, hate, jealousy, envy, anger, resentment.

The desires are feelings of need that must be fulfilled for a person to have the greatest level of health and well being and include physical desires (for food, water, shelter, sex, sleep, and rest) and cognitive desires (such as for freedom, happiness, knowledge, power and approval).

Although we know that the soul and spirit exist separately from each other (I Thessalonians 5:23), in actuality they are so closely related that it is often extremely difficult to distinguish between them. Hebrews 4:12 says that it takes the Word of God to separate them.

BODY

The body is the part of you that is world or SENSE-conscious. It is governed by nature or natural laws.

The body is the temple or house of the soul and spirit. It is how we contact and interact with the world around us, including other people and our physical environment. It operates by and houses the five senses.

We've known about the senses from childhood, but consider the special ways that they interact and affect us.

- Sight—The ability to identify or perceive objects with the eye. About 80 percent of what we learn comes through our eyes. Our eyes perceive light, project images inwardly, and send messages to the brain faster than the blink of an eye, registering about 864,000 visual messages each day.

- Hearing—The ability to perceive and distinguish sounds with the ear. The eardrum detects vibrations caused by changing air pressure and converts that to sound. Parts of the ear are sensitive to gravity and acceleration and help our sense of balance.

- Smell—The ability to perceive the presence of odors with the nose. The quickest way to produce an emotional response is with smell. Smell is also responsible for 90 percent of our sense of taste.

- Touch—The ability to register physical contact. Touch is important to our overall welfare. Studies indicate that babies can die from the lack of nurturing touch.

- Taste—The ability to experience flavors with the mouth. It's no accident that babies put everything in their mouths. Our instincts guide us to experience quite a bit of our world through the mouth.

We are strongly influenced by our senses. God created us this way. The Word says that we are "fearfully and wonderfully made." Our body and soul, the seat of our personality and actions, are ruled by self and natural laws, and are without the governance of God unless our spirits become involved. The Word calls this natural human nature without God, our flesh.

Now, we are most familiar with the operation of our physical body because it is tangible and visible, whereas our soul and spirit are not. We are more in control of our bodies because basically, the body simply acts as it is directed by the soul; by our mind, emotions, and will.

We have more trouble controlling our souls —our thoughts and feelings. Our spirits are in darkness or spiritually dead until we are born again, and then must be developed through the Word of God, prayer, and communion with Him. We are least familiar with and least used to operating on this level of our being. For most people, the body and soul are in control and govern our lives.

This is in direct opposition to the way we were created by God to function, and is the underlying reason behind most of our problems, even when we are born again. Have you ever wondered why, even though you are saved and filled with God's Spirit, you still struggle with habits, thoughts, uncontrollable urges and longings, and find yourself caught in situations and actions you know are not pleasing to God and that bring you nothing but grief?

Why is it that, as the Apostle Paul so aptly puts it, we do the evil things that we don't want to do, but the good and right things we want to do, we don't do (Romans 7:19)? He goes on to explain that there is a *law in our members* that wars against our spirits. (Romans 7:20, 23) However God, Who created us with this three-fold nature, has given us a command and a promise. The command is *Walk in the Spirit...*and the promise is that if we do, we ...*shall not fulfill the lust of the flesh.* (Galatians 5:16) In other words, we will not fall prey to sin and destructive behaviors. Rather, we reap the benefits of abundant life.

Remember, we were originally created to be governed by our spirits indwelt by the Spirit of God. When we leave the order and plan established by God, we find ourselves in deep trouble. The problems that stem from abandoning God's ways do not affect just us, for it is a spiritual truth that what we do affects many generations to come. (Deuteronomy 29:14, 15; Exodus 34:7,20:5) We can see the devastation that these destructive behaviors leave in their wake: wasted lives, mental and physical abuse, disease, torn families, and damaged children.

That is why God solemnly commands us to teach His precepts and His commands to our children, that they may in turn pass this knowledge on to future generations. (Deuteronomy 6:2, 5-9) We can't say, "It's nobody's business but mine" when we decide to do our own thing. We can't say, "I'm not hurting anyone but myself." It simply is not true. The story of Mephibosheth reveals how our choices affect our children and generations to come. It was because of choices made by his grand-father, King Saul, that Mephibosheth found himself in such a predicament. While he languished in Lo-debar, however, the Holy Spirit worked through past actions of the young man's father, Jonathan, to change his life.

Mephibosheth's grandfather, King Saul, started out serving God, but gradually turned away from Him. As he drifted in rebellion and anger, Saul hated David and tried to kill him; nevertheless, David and Saul's son, Jonathan, had a remarkable friendship. Jonathan recognized David as the future king and entered into covenant with him. David promised that when he became king he would always show kindness toward Jonathan's family. (1 Samuel 20:13-16).

Years after Saul and Jonathan died, David remem-bered his promise. He asked a servant about any living members of Jonathan's family. The servant told him about Mephibosheth. King David summoned him to not only come to his house, but to become a part of his household. The King said: *You shall eat bread at my table continually.*

Mephibosheth could have decided to refuse David's invitation out of unbelief, or pride, fear and anger because of his situation. But he didn't, and so the cripple came to dwell with the king. Mephibosheth's decision mirrors the decision we must make as God, in His infinite love and mercy, beckons us to sit at His table. In all honesty, we know that we are undeserving. We too often dwell in what we can see, hear, think and feel, instead of in His will.

However, God is ready and willing to forgive us. He will erase the shame and degradation of our past and receive us with open arms. He is prepared to restore us to the original purpose for our lives.

A Prayer for Direction

Lord, Adonai

In self, many times I have made choices out of
desperation which brought devastation to me,
and those around me,
because Your spirit did not govern me.
Today, I renounce my flesh-ruled life, that has
influenced me negatively,
and I seek your original plan for my life.
Today, I choose to be God-conscious as I hope
and wait in you.
Show me what I lack to be clear in my mind,
what I am to do,
and the truth I am to know concerning Your
plan for my life.

Life Gates:
Entrances to the
Body, Soul and Spirit

CHAPTER 2

Life Gates:
Entrances to Body, Soul and Spirit

When we turn away from God, we turn away from the commandments He's given us and the structure He has established for our lives. We decide to go around the boundaries He has set up and throw off the restraints He has put in place for our protection, and do things our way instead. Then we reap trouble for ourselves, our families, future generations, and even our nations.

God's plan is for us to enjoy the fruit of the spirit in our lives. These inner treasures are:

> *Love, joy (gladness), peace, patience (an even temper, forbearance), kindness, goodness (benevolence), faithfulness, meekness (humility), gentleness, self-control.*
> *Galatians 5:22, 23 (AMP)*

Instead, many people are caught up in destructive behaviors and don't know how to get free. They feel helpless, and most don't understand why they can't seem to stop doing the very things that they know are destroying them and their families.

But there is hope. And that hope lies in gaining an understanding of the truth about why we do the things we do, and how to make positive life changes. That truth is found in a concept we call *Life Gates*.

Life Gates: Entrance to Body, Soul and Spirit

Just about everything we experience in life is experienced through one of our senses, which we are going to call "gates." They are entrances to our physical, soul, and spirit realms. You see, these gates or entrances exist on all three levels of our being, but they function differently according to the design and purpose of the various parts of our being.

The physical senses—sight, hearing, smell, touch, taste—are simply how we gather or take in information about our surroundings. They don't apply value judgments to the information; there's no positive or negative, good or bad connected to what the physical senses register. They are neutral. For instance, our eye sees a flower and it registers that physical fact, but it does not make the judgment of whether the flower is pretty, desirable or what to do with it. Those distinctions and decisions are made on the soul and spirit level. Your body just gathers the information.

All information received by the physical senses is filtered through another set of sense gates: those of the soul. The soul is our agent for processing and interpreting the information coming through the physical sense gates, and determining what we choose to do or how we direct the body to react or respond to the information.

When our soul gates get involved, our mind, with its thoughts and reasoning, emotions and feelings, as well as our will all begin to play a part. Let's go back to the example of the flower we saw with our physical eyes. As the information enters the soul gate, our feelings and emotions add to the information already stored up by our mind about the flower, and the eyes of our soul perceives beauty. Desire may be kindled and the thought arises to possess the flower. Our will may then send a signal to our body to react—to cut the flower and take it home.

Now, if the flower is in your neighbor's yard, or in a florist's shop, that may not be such a good decision. This is a simple example, but it illustrates the trouble we can get into by allowing the body and soul to act on their own, without proper direction and oversight. This oversight was intended by God to be provided by our regenerated spirit, a spirit committed to God. If the person in the example would follow his spirit's leading, it would restrain the will from commissioning and the body from committing a wrong act. All of these processes are happening in mini-seconds, all at once, subconsciously.

Let's take another example. In a conversation, someone says something that offends you. The sounds of the words picked up by your physical ears are in themselves neutral. But the problem arises in the realm of your soul as you interpret the words in accordance with your thoughts and emotions. Your thoughts also may contain past memories and experiences that come into play. Then your will determines how to react. Will you retaliate with hurtful words of your own? Will you internalize your interpretation and allow yourself to become bound by the words? Jesus said, *"Take heed what you hear."* (Mark 4:24). Some translations say, *"Take heed how you hear."* In other words, we need to carefully regulate how our soul (mind and emotions) is interpreting, and how our will reacts to the information we receive.

You can see how very far-reaching and critical the governance and proper regulation of our soul gates become. The soul is so intricate and has such potential power for good or evil that it is of vital importance that God regulates its operation. The soul and body can go haywire without proper control. That is why we are admonished in the Scriptures to, *"..take every thought captive to the obedience of Christ."* (2 Corinthians 10:5) The Amplified Bible states it this way, *"...refute arguments and theories and reasonings and every proud and lofty thing that sets itself up against the [true] knowledge of God; and ...lead every thought and purpose away captive into the obedience of Christ..."*

In other words, don't automatically accept every thought or feeling that arises within you, but instead examine them in the light of God's truth. The information that enters our sense gates on the physical and soulical level must be filtered through the spirit senses if we are to walk in truth and respond to every situation in the right way. We are to measure all things by the Word of God, not by how we think or feel. The mind of man is a battle-field where Satan and his evil spirits war against the Word of God and against our faith. Every temptation, which Satan uses to trap us, is first presented to the mind. Satan uses our flesh to secure the consent of our will. In each instance of temptation, the enemy presents some kind of thought to entice us.

The emotions and desires are motivators that when activated, can spur us on to actions that are de-structive if our feelings are not brought under the scrutiny and control of the spirit.

> *Each one is tempted when he is drawn away by his own desires and enticed. Then, when desire has conceived, it gives birth to sin; and sin, when it is full-grown, brings forth death. Do not be deceived….*
> **James 1:14-16 (NKJV)**

The chain reaction of sin generally follows this

pattern. The thought is presented to your mind, then your feelings (desires) become involved. If your thoughts and desires are contrary to what is good and are not checked, you will choose an improper course of action. We were created to live and operate in the spirit, not in the flesh. The flesh is the lower nature of man, it is the soul and body without the governing agency of the recreated spirit.

Unfortunately, most people, most of the time, operate only from these two levels of their nature: soul and body. But this is not how God intended it to be! Our spirits were meant to be the covering and regulator for our soulical and physical natures. Our spirits, indwelt by the Spirit of God, are meant to control and govern our souls and bodies. Our spirit is designed by God to rightly discern the information we receive through both our physical and soul gates. It is the spirit that gives the information its correct meaning, purpose, and application, and determines the right course of action for us.

"What would Jesus do?" became a popular slogan not long ago. The answer is simple. Jesus said He always did that which pleased the Father. (John 8:2) The Spirit always led him. God's wisdom and knowledge are available to us as we walk in the spirit, and not in the flesh.

The Principle of Sense Gates in Scripture

The Bible offers many examples of our natural and spiritual senses in operation.

Sight

> *...So when the woman [Eve] saw that the tree was good for food, that it was pleasant to the eyes, and a tree desirable to make one wise, she took of its fruit and ate. She also gave to her husband with her, and he ate. Then the eyes of both of them were opened, and they knew that they were naked...*
>
> *Genesis 3:6, 7 (NKJV)*

Eve "saw" that the tree was good. The Word says it was pleasant to her eyes, a desirable thing, so she took of the fruit, ate, and gave some to her husband, Adam. Then, verse seven tells us that the eyes of both of them were opened and they knew that they were naked.

Now, we know that their physical eyes were open before this happened, and they were naked all along. But now their eyes were opened on another level of their being. Their souls became aware of shame as they "saw" themselves differently now. If they had still been in fellowship with God and still had spiritual sight, their reaction to what they "saw" would have been different.

But their spiritual eye gate had been darkened.

In 2 Kings 6:15-17, we find another example of sight, this time on the spiritual level. The prophet Elisha's servant Gehazi was distressed when he saw the army of the enemy poised against him and his master. "What are we going to do?" he asked. Then the prophet prayed that God would open Gehazi's eyes. His servant needed to see the truth. When the Lord opened Gehazi's (spiritual) eyes, he saw that the mountain was full of horses and chariots of fire, protecting them. Your natural eyes may only see what is apparent, but your spiritual eyes, enlightened by God's Spirit, will see what is true.

Hearing

"He who has an ear, let him hear what the Spirit says..." If you are going to rightly discern what you hear, you must open up your spiritual ears. You cannot hear what the Spirit says with your natural ears, and you cannot always trust the ears of the soul to give you a correct interpretation of the words you hear. If that was possible, no one would ever believe lies or gossip, and there would be no misunderstandings between people. These things happen because what is heard is received only on the physical and soul levels, and never reaches the spiritual ears.

King Hezekiah heard distressing news when the King of Assyria sent him a message demanding Jerusalem's surrender and boasting of the lands that Assyria had conquered and destroyed. If he had heard with just his natural and soulish ears, he would have been tempted to give up in fear. But King Hezekiah did what always brings victory, he sought God and listened for directions with his spiritual ears. He processed the information through his spiritual ear gate. When he followed God's instructions, the nation was delivered (2 Kings 19).

Smell

Do you like the smell of spice potpourri? Many people do, but some think it stinks. What makes the perception of its smell different for different people? While there may be differences in our nasal structure, the major difference undoubtedly lies in our souls. And while smelling potpourri is harmless enough, there are other instances in which having a spiritual nose is essential.

From the time of Moses, the children of Israel offered sacrifices in obedience to the Lord. The smell of the sacrifice must have said to them that they were doing God's will. In Isaiah 1:13, however, God tells Israel to bring no more futile sacrifices and says that the smell of their incense is an abomination to Him, because they had drifted from doing His will. What may smell good to us can be a stench in God's nostrils. It would be wise to know the difference. Only those who operate in the spirit would be able to differentiate.

Touch

> *Now a woman, having a flow of blood for twelve years, who had spent all her livelihood on physicians and could not be healed by any, came from behind and touched the border of His garment. And immediately her flow of blood stopped. And Jesus said, 'Who touched me?' For I perceived power going out from Me.*
>
> *Luke 8:43-46 (NKJV)*

This familiar story illustrates an important point about the power of touch. But it is not speaking of touch on just the natural or soul levels. The woman touched Jesus with her faith. She was operating in the spirit. Just touching Jesus naturally or even emotionally would not have brought her healing. After all, many in the crowd were touching Him. It was through the spiritual touch that deliverance came.

In 1 Samuel 10:26 the Word speaks of *"men whose hearts God had touched."* Does this mean they actually felt

God's physical touch? Not very likely. Neither is it talking about an emotional feeling. But there is a sense in which you know that God has touched you—in the spirit. If you are not sensitive to the spirit, and live only on the physical and soul levels, you will fail to recognize and receive God's touch. And it is His touch that heals.

Taste

In two instances, Ezekiel 3: 1-3 and Revelation 10:9, 10, the Lord instructed prophets to eat the Word. In both cases, the word was sweet in their mouths, but once swallowed, it was bitter. Learning about God can be delightful, but applying His truths can disagree with our fleshly nature.

Psalm 34:8 invites us to *'taste'* and *'see'* that the Lord is good. And Psalm 119:103 declares that God's words are *"sweet to the taste, sweeter than honey."* Many people simply look at these scriptures as figures of speech, knowing that one cannot taste God or words in the natural, but there is a very real sense in which we can taste God in the spirit.

Touch and taste are senses that are used in our most intimate experiences. As we worship God, we are getting intimate with Him. In the Greek, one of the meanings of worship is "to kiss toward." Kissing is an intimate expression of love and affection. You could say it is "tasting" of a person. Worshipping God is tasting Him in the spirit.

Through worship and intimate communion with God, we experience Him and taste His goodness, His mercy, His grace, and His love. James 3:11 asks a pertinent question: *"Can bitter and sweet, cursing and blessing come out of the same mouth?"* This cannot be when we walk in the spirit. But living according to the flesh brings contradiction and confusion. We cannot taste the things of God and things of the world and expect to reap blessings.

<u>Walking in the Spirit</u>

On the spirit level, people often talk of a "sixth" sense. They call it intuition, or having a hunch. This is an area that is receiving a lot of attention today, because people are searching for something more than what they can see, hear, and know on a natural level. So, we see many turning to psychics, mediums, fortune-tellers, astrologers, and other occult practitioners. They know that there is more to life than what they are experiencing, but they don't know how to find it. What they are looking for is life more abundant, and that is only found in Jesus Christ.

In God's original design, the power of the soul was completely under the control of the spirit. When man sinned, the Bible states he died spiritually—he lost his ability to hear, sense, or respond to God's Spirit. His soul gradually gained the upper hand and began to dominate the spirit. Man became flesh ruled (controlled or governed by his desires and passions.) Romans 12:2 exhorts us, '*to be transformed (from living flesh-ruled lives) by the renewing of our mind.*' This is the process by which we reverse the dominant order and function of the soul. It is accomplished by receiving the engrafted Word of God through the spirit.

Our ability to hear, sense and respond to God's Spirit lies in our regenerated spirit. When we are born again and God's Spirit comes to live in our spirit, our gates of the spirit that were locked shut by sin are opened once again. We are able to "see" the Lord, and distinguish His Hand at work; to "hear" His voice, receive His word and obey Him; to "smell" the sweet fragrance of His presence; and to "touch" and "taste" Him.

An unregenerated person's spirit has lost its ability

to sense, hear, and respond to the Spirit of God.
According to Ephesians 2:1 such a person is spiritually
dead. This person's spirit is dead to God, but it may
remain as active as the mind and be stronger than the
soul when under demonic influence.

We are seeing more and more of this kind of
activity as people yield themselves, knowingly or unknow-
ingly, to the seductive claims of New Age beliefs, astrol-
ogy, psychics, mediums, clairvoyants, witchcraft, and
other brands of supposed enlightenment. Unfortunately,
they don't understand that they are allowing stimuli from
the kingdom of darkness to enter their gates, and that
their souls, spirits, and bodies are at the very least being
negatively influenced and at worst are being brought into
satanic domination and bondage.

In 1 Timothy 4:1 (NKJV) God warns us,

> *Now the Spirit expressly says that in
> latter times some will depart from the
> faith, giving heed to deceiving spirits
> and doctrines of demons, speaking lies
> in hypocrisy...*

And in 2 Timothy 4:3, 4 (NKJV) we are told,

> *For the time will come when they will
> not endure sound doctrine but accord
> ing to their own desires, because*

*they have itching ears, they will heap
up for themselves teachers; and they
will turn their ears away from the truth,
and be turned aside to fables.*

The Word of God and our spirit, indwelt by the Spirit of God, give us access to Truth. There is no truth to be found any other way or in any other avenue. Our first response must always be to turn to God for wisdom and direction.

The "sixth sense" people desire to experience is simply living and walking in the Spirit as God originally intended for man to do. When we operate on the spirit level, having our bodies and souls in subjection to the Spirit of God, being led and guided by our Creator, we experience discernment, the ability to 'know' through our spiritual senses—sight, hearing, smell, touch, and taste—that which can be known in no other way. Discernment is the result of the spiritual gates of man being open to receive from the Spirit of God. The information that comes through discernment is not picked up by our natural senses; it must be furnished by the Spirit of God and detected in our spiritual senses.

Our spiritual senses, as we have seen, also function as the means for taking the information from the physical and soul senses and giving it the right meaning, purpose, and application. So, we see that operating on the spirit level—walking in the Spirit—is essential if we are going to live successful, productive, blessed lives and have the prosperous relationships with God and others that God intended for us when He first created man.

The Word of God alludes in many instances to the senses or gates of the body, soul and spirit. These gates affect every aspect of our lives. All of our relationships, with God and others, are experienced through these gates. Our relationship with God takes place on the spirit level. We are to worship God in spirit and in truth. He speaks to our spirit and lives in our spirit, but He is interested in all of the levels of our being and wants us to allow His Spirit to govern us completely.

Giving the Holy Spirit charge over our sense gates is extremely important when it comes to our relationships with others. All of our senses become activated when we begin to experience another person. In relationships, we also desire the other person to experience us. So there is a giving and receiving that takes place on all three levels of our being—spirit, soul, and body. Just how each individual orchestrates that giving and receiving on each level makes all the difference in the relationship, and also determines if it is a godly, mutually beneficial one, or is ungodly, and destructive.

We can all recount stories of destructive relationships. Perhaps you are involved in one yourself right now. You may be wondering what happened, how you got to the place you find yourself now. It may be a painful place, a frightening place, and a place that seems hopeless. You may think there's no way out of your situation. But here is a message of hope. There is a way out. There can be restoration of your body, soul, and spirit. It is through the Lord Jesus Christ. There is a balm in Gilead. But you must be willing to reach out and receive it, even through the pain.

A Prayer of Enlightenment

The Lord our Righteousness: Jehovah Tsidkenu

I cast off every work of darkness I have allowed
to enter into my gates through ignorance.
Thank you for the truth of who I am,
the truth of why I was created,
and the truth that exposes Satan's lies.
Today, I yield my senses to You
Lord, for Your glory.
Thank You that my gates are no longer locked nor
blocked, but open to the leading of the Holy Spirit.
Today, I walk by faith and not by sight, first seeking
the wisdom and direction of God.

Spirit Life Gauge

A Self Evaluation

My Spirit Life Gauge

Take some time to get an honest picture of your life.

SPIRIT

1. Percent of time spent in communion with the Father God.

   _____ Prayer

   _____ Praise and worship

   _____ Thanksgiving

   _____ Church

   _____ Reading and studying the Word

   _____ Percent of time spent on other activities.

   (List your favorite activities)

2. Do you mostly give, or seek to receive?

3. Do you serve with an unassuming spirit or seek recognition?

4. Do you obey the leading of the Holy Spirit or your own inclinations?

5. Do you examine your own heart motives?

SOUL

Mind

1. Do you entertain thoughts you shouldn't? In what areas?

2. Do you seek to renew your mind with the Word of God, or fill it with things of the world?

Emotions

1. Do you allow doubt, fear, or discouragement to overtake you?

2. Do you succumb to irrational anger, jealousy, envy, covetousness, pride, or other ungodly feelings?

3. What do you set your affections on? What things/people have first place in your emotions?

Will

1. When faced with a decision, do you find out what the Word of God says first?

2. Do you have a teachable spirit or are you headstrong?

3. When you know God's will do you still do your own thing?

BODY: SENSE GATES

Sight

1. Do you allow your eyes to look at things they shouldn't?

2. Do you read material that you know is not appropriate?

3. Do you spend an inordinate amount of time looking at television or going to movies?

Hearing

1. Do you lend your ears to listen to things they shouldn't, such as gossip, slander, evil reports, dirty talk, ungodly music?

2. Do you make hearing the Word of God a priority in your life?

Taste

1.   Do you taste (partake) of things that you shouldn't, such as liquor, cigarettes, illegal drugs, and unlawful kisses?

2.   Do you use your organ of taste (mouth) as a vehicle for ungodly words (lies, gossip, etc.)?

Smell

1.   Do you allow your nose to experience smells that may lead you into ungodly behavior?

Touch

1.   Do your hands touch anything they shouldn't? Are you involved in any practice that is not pleasing to God?

2.   Do you extend your hands to help people?

3.   Do you use your hands to hurt others?

> *Do not yield your members as servants*
> *of unrighteousness, but rather yield*
> *them as servants to righteousness.*
> **Romans 6:13**

Stories of Loss and Recovery

CHAPTER 3

Stories of Loss and Recovery

God has placed treasures inside each of us, treasures of great value. Some of these inner treasures are special giftings and others include the fruit that comes with His indwelling Spirit: humility, patience, love, faith, gentleness, peace, joy, self-control, and longsuffering.

But what happens when we allow our souls to take precedence over our spirits? Our treasures get buried or hidden, caught up in the emotions of pain, rejection, pride, shame, anger, guilt, fear, and desperation.

The following two stories of Tamar and Amnon and of the Shunammite woman are stories of people just like you and me. As their stories unfold, you will see and feel their experiences. You will see some treasures that were lost, some found, and some never regained.

Before going to the next page, stop and reflect on what may be your hidden treasures.

Stories of Loss and Recovery

The Bible presents vivid accounts of how the enemy can subtly bring about destruction in our lives. How we react to a life crisis determines our victory or devastation. If we are led by our physical senses (what we see, hear, touch, etc), or by our soul (mind, will and emotions) we will fall. If we submit our senses to God's Spirit, we will overcome.

Let's look at two biblical stories that show how our choices determine our outcome. In each case, the person did not deserve the emotional or physical pains they endured. One sunk into despair while the other emerged victorious.

The first story is that of a young girl named Tamar. She was the daughter of King David, the most powerful king in all Israel. Tamar was beautiful, vibrant, kindhearted and the epitome of a young, royal virgin. Although only fifteen, Tamar already walked in the custom of young women of her day. Her richly colored robe was an outward portrayal of her position—a princess with a bright and prosperous future. She knew who she was and to whom she belonged. Tamar was of marriageable age, and true to the custom of that day, she was kept under close surveillance. Imagine having everything at

your fingertips: beauty, position and prestige. Her very
name describes her strength, stability, and character.
"Tamar" means "palm tree."

Tamar had God-given qualities such as character,
innocence, purity, dignity, respect, self esteem, gracious-
ness, humility, freedom, and she had family connections.
Who wouldn't want these attributes? Unfortunately,
Tamar's story takes a tragic turn.

In 2 Samuel 13, we are told of Tamar's half-
brother Amnon and the obsession he developed for his
sister. Any noble attributes Amnon might have had were
overcome by his fleshly desire. Over a period of time, he
longed for Tamar sexually to the point of making himself
physically sick. Have you ever wanted something so bad
that you couldn't eat or sleep? Your time is consumed,
day and night, longing for that person or thing.

Jonadab, Amnon's crafty cousin, became concerned about Amnon's brooding which was causing him
to lose weight. Amnon confessed his desire for his sister,
Tamar. Jonadab proceeded to devise a plot to help his
friend satisfy his lustful passion. The plan that Jonadab
encouraged Amnon to carry out was to first pretend to be
sick then to ask his father the king to allow his young
sister to come prepare food in his sight and feed him.

When the king came to see his son, he saw his illness and had no reason to suspect a plot. After all, several servants were present, so Tamar would not be alone with Amnon, which was against the custom for a virgin. The king gave his consent and sent for Tamar to come to Amnon's house and do as he requested. Tamar had no reason to be suspicious of her half-brother's request or question the instructions of her father, especially since he was the one who sent for her. You know how it is when you make a sandwich for your ailing brother and he asks you to bring it to him; you think nothing of it.

As Amnon watched Tamar make the cakes, his desire for her increased. When she finished preparing the cakes she presented them to him, but he refused to eat. He sent all the servants away and requested Tamar to bring the food into his bedchambers.

Amnon's diabolical scheme was working. Tamar was right where he wanted her: vulnerable, open, and available. Just as a leopard stalks his prey and lies in wait until the opportune time to pounce, Amnon was lying in wait to devour Tamar to satisfy his insatiable lust. Tamar took the food into the bedchamber for Amnon to eat and to her horror he grabbed her. If we do not master our passions, our passions will master us. Amnon said,

> *...Come to bed with me my sister. Tamar*
> *responds, don't my brother!, don't force me.*
> *Such a thing should not be done in Israel.*
> *Don't do this wicked thing. What about me:*
> *Where could I get rid of my disgrace? And*
> *what about you? You would be like one of the*
> *wicked fools in Israel. Please speak to the*
> *king; he will not keep me from being married*
> *to you.*
>
> **2 Samuel 13:11-13 (TLB)**

But like many of us, in the throes of passion Amnon disregarded sound advice. Have you ever felt like Tamar, paralyzed with fear, trying to find a way of escape? Tamar could not escape Amnon's violence. He raped her. To add insult to injury, afterward he no longer referred to her as Tamar, but *this woman*. He demanded that his servants pick her up, put her out of his house, and bolt the door!

Can you imagine the devastation, the humiliation, the pain and anger she must have felt? Everything that was so positive in her life, all of her God-given treasures, seemed lost in a few moments. Tamar's heart was shattered into a thousand pieces. Feeling ripped, torn, ugly, embarrassed, ruined and ashamed, she could no longer hold her head up with pride. Surely everyone would know of the hideous evil her brother had just exacted upon her.

She was in such anguish that she ripped her robe of many colors, laid her head in her hands, and went away crying bitterly.

In her condition of devastation, Tamar made her way to her brother Absalom's house. He seemed to know, intuitively, that Amnon had defiled her. His attention went immediately to revenge rather than to comforting his sister. We are never told that Tamar called upon the Lord in her despair. 2 Samuel 13:19, 20 says,

> *And Tamar put ashes on her head, and rent her garment of divers colors that was on her, and laid her hand on her head and went on crying. And Absalom her brother said unto 'Her, Hath Amnon thy brother been with thee? But hold now thy peace, my sister: he is thy brother; regard not this thing.' So Tamar remained desolate in her brother Absalom's house.*

Thus Tamar ended up partnering with death instead of reaching out for life. She remained desolate in Absalom's house.

If Tamar had only understood how much God cares for us then she could have reaped the benefits of

Jeremiah 29:11 which tells us that the Lord's plans for us are for good, not for evil, plans for our prosperity and not our harm. She would have known that what the enemy meant for evil, God can turn to good. Perhaps she would have looked to God for direction instead of her brother. We're not promised that we won't suffer hardships and heartaches, but trying situations should move us to call on God for whatever we need.

Tamar was violated on all three levels of her being: spirit, soul, and body. Her body was assaulted, her soul was bruised, and her spirit was crushed. She never recovered. Her answer lay in opening up her spiritual gates to the Lord and receiving from Him. If she had been able to hear His voice, see His hand at work, be healed by His touch, and taste His unconditional love, it would have ministered to her soul. The desolation, shame, hurt, fear, and hopelessness she felt and thought was her lot, could have been overcome. Her story would have had a different ending.

Our minds, wills, and emotions are involved in our decision-making process. Every choice we make produces fruit of some kind. Is it possible that Tamar gave up? Obviously, she had no hope. Shame had overtaken her very soul; in her eyes she no longer had a future. The rape by her brother did not make her any less the daughter of the king. However, when we make decisions based in the flesh, we open the door to our own destruction.

According to 1 Corinthians 10:11, everything in the Word is written for our example. God did not want Tamar to remain desolate. He gave us the ability to choose. In *He Loves Me He Loves Me Not*, *(p. 78-79)* [1] Paula White tells of her early life of sexual abuse, family history of suicide, and sexual immorality before coming to Christ. She said,

> *Pain can become a conduit for power...What was meant to destroy us can actually be what makes us strong and whole. What was supposed to be a stumbling block in our life can actually become a stepping stone. ...God communes with, blesses, and uses people, not because they are perfect in life, but because they painfully discovered the way of grace. God does his most power ful work when we are weak, empty and helpless. This is not the state we like to be in, but it is the condition out of which God builds masterpieces.*

If only Tamar could have taken hold of this truth. Your life may be empty and broken right now, but it is not the end for you. It is merely an opportunity for God to move. He can move, bring order and do a miraculous, creative work in your life.

If we will trust Him rather than give in to our circumstances, God is able to bring life out of our dead, desolate situations. A case in point is the Old Testament account of another woman who, like Tamar, found herself in horrendous circumstances. The story of the Shunammite woman is found in 2 Kings 4.

A woman of means, the Shunammite graciously cared for the prophet Elisha whenever he came to her city. In return for her generosity, the prophet announced that she would bear a son. This was good news indeed, for the woman was childless and her husband was old. No doubt she was overwhelmed by the pronouncement, because she replied to the prophet, "Please, don't lie to me." Nevertheless, at the appointed time her son was born.

This miracle child must have been a source of great joy to the Shunammite and her husband. Surely he was one of the treasures of her life. But one day, while helping his father in the fields, the boy was stricken ill. Several hours later, he died in his mother's arms.

Can you imagine the shock, horror and grief she must have felt? How utterly devastated at this cruel turn of events? What would she do? Her soul must have been in torment, her emotions ravaged. It would have been easy, and even expected, to give up in defeat and despair. After all, her child was dead. Her treasure was gone. Tamar would have known how she felt.

But here this woman's story diverges from Tamar's. Instead of accepting the seeming hopelessness of her circumstances and choosing to remain desolate, the Shunammite refused to give in to her emotions or even to what her physical senses were telling her. She refused to allow her circumstances to dictate her future.

Without wasting any time in despondency or self-pity, she went to where she knew there was help for her situation. She went after God with a passion. *"Then she saddled an ass, and said to her servant, Drive, and go forward; slack not thy riding for me...." (v.24)* The Shunammite woman's response to her situation was to go forward! She refused to remain desolate in her circumstance. She arose and went to the man of God. When she was asked if everything was all right, her reply vividly showed that her eyes were focused on something other than the physical evidence.

> **So she went and came unto the man of God to mount Carmel. And it came to pass, when**

> *the man of God saw her afar off, that he said*
> *to Gehazi, his servant, ' Behold, yonder is that*
> *Shunammite: Run now, I pray thee, to meet*
> *her, and say unto her, Is it well with thee? Is it*
> *well with thy husband? Is it well with the*
> *child?' And she answered, ' It is well.' (vs. 25,*
> *26)*

She said that all was well, even though her son lay lifeless. And when she had told him what happened, the prophet came home with her.

> *And when Elisha was come into the house,*
> *behold, the child was dead, and laid up on his*
> *bed. He went in therefore, and shut the door*
> *upon them twain, and prayed unto the Lord.*
> *And he went up and lay upon the child, and*
> *put his mouth upon his mouth, and his eyes*
> *upon his eyes; and his hands upon his hands:*
> *and he stretched himself upon the child; and*
> *the flesh of the child waxed warm. Then he*
> *returned, and walked in the house to and fro;*
> *and went up, and stretched himself upon him:*
> *and the child sneezed seven times, and the*
> *child opened his eyes. And he called Gehazi*
> *[his servant] and said, 'Call this Shunammite.'*
> *So he called her. And when she was come in*
> *unto him, he said, 'Take up thy son. (vs. 32-*
> *36).*

As a result, in response to her faith and trust, and because she did not allow her soul with its raging emotions to reign unchecked, but chose to see with the eyes of her spirit, her son was restored to her alive. Her treasure was not lost after all! *"God is able to do exceeding abundantly, above all that we ask or think, according to the power that is at work in us,"* the power that is unleashed as we walk in the spirit and not in the flesh.

Isn't God good? If we believe God can turn things around, He will restore our joy. The Shunammite woman regained her treasure. Tamar lost hers. The Shunammite allowed her spirit to overcome her fear. The pain of her emotions consumed Tamar.

When we hang on to our excuses, however justified they seem, and choose to remain desolate, we become insecure, fearful, full of pain, rage, anger and pride. We hang on to the shame of our past, which can paralyze the present. Living in the past will rob you of your future and destiny. We should stand on the Word in Isaiah 50:5, which says, *"The Lord has opened my ears and I was not rebellious, nor did I turn away. And the seventh verse says, "...the Lord will help me and I will not be disgraced. Therefore, I set my face like a flint and I know that I will not be ashamed."*

We do not have to be deceitful like Amnon, nor do we have to remain desolate like Tamar. We don't even have to live as an evil craftsman like Jonadab. Maybe Tamar never heard of God's power to change her life, but you have. This book brings the message to you. Here's your invitation. God invites you to come out of desolation and enjoy abundant life.

1. Taken from "He Loves Me He Loves Me Not" by Paula White. *Used by permission of* Paula White. Creation House
www.paulawhite.org

A Prayer for Healing

The Lord that Heals: Jehovah Rapha

In my pain, hurt, pride, and feelings of rejection, I had
forgotten the benefits You said were mine.
But today, with new understanding, I receive all the
blessings and benefits that come with being whole.
Forgive me, Lord, for staying too long in my desolate
place, and not first seeking and trusting You.
Today, I choose to forgive those who caused me pain.
Today I also choose to live.
Open my heart that I might receive Your plans for me,
plans for good, for a future, and a hope.
Thank You that no weapon formed against
me shall prosper.
Father, help me to discover in Your Word, the treasure
You have placed within me.

Generations:
Guardians of Our Children's Gates

Chapter 4

Generations :
Guardians of Our Children's Gates

The problems that stem from abandoning God's ways do not affect just us, for it is a spiritual truth that what we do affects many generations to come.

> *The Lord God...keeping mercy for thousands, forgiving iniquity and transgression and sin, and that will by no means clear the guilty; visiting the iniquity of the fathers upon the children, and upon the children's children, unto the third and to the fourth generation.*
> *Exodus 34:7*

It is clear that God has charged parents with the important task of being godly examples and guardians of their children's gates by teaching them the principles and commandments from the Word of God.

> *And these words, which I command thee this day, shall be in thine heart: and thou shall teach them diligently unto thy children, and shall talk of them when thou sittest in thine house, and when thou walkest by the way, and when thou liest down, and when thou risest up. And thou shall bind them for a sign upon thine hand, and they shall be as frontlets between thine eyes. And thou shall write them upon the posts of thy house, and on the gates.*
> *Deuteronomy 6: 5-9*

> *Train up a child in the way he should*
> *go: and when he is old, he will not*
> *depart from it.*
>
> **Proverbs 22:6**

How did generational curses begin? It started
when man chose sin and departed from God's ways. If
we would go back to the ancient paths (God's commandments), generational curses will be broken. Parents must
choose wisdom and obedience. We can take authority
over the devil, and over every demonic spirit and bind
them from our children forever; by learning and walking in
the principles God has already set before us.

Generations: Guardians of Our Children's Gates

Parents are to pass on the teachings and love for God's Word to their children. Each generation should become stronger in the Word than the preceding one; however, everything around us paints a different picture. It is as true today as it was in the Old Testament.

Even Christian parents, who know how to go to God themselves, often have not been as diligent in passing this knowledge on to their children. The story of Tamar, daughter of King David, is a good example of what happens when parents fail to pass on godly moral standards and precepts to their offspring.

Tamar, through no fault of her own, is brutality raped by her brother, Amnon, and sinks into utter desolation. In despair she turns to her brother Absalom, in whose house she takes refuge. However, we never read of her calling on God or seeking solace in Him. Could it have been that King David never taught Tamar how to go to God for direction and help?

We have cause to question David's teaching to his children when we read that Tamar remained in desolation. Then we learn that when David heard of the incident, he was disturbed but did not exact due punishment on his son, Amnon. As a result, Absalom avenged his sister's rape by killing Amnon two years later. David was a man who knew and loved the Lord yet we see his offsprings' lives in ruin.

The Word of God tells us in Exodus 34:7 that, the iniquity of fathers is visited upon their children unto the third and fourth generations. It is interesting to note that the same pattern of lust and murder that we see in David's life is repeated in the lives of his children. There are many modern day examples of such generational curses.

One case is of a family that produced five generations, each following in the destructive pattern set by their forebearers of promiscuity, children out of wedlock, manipulation and deceit. Such behaviors only grow stronger as they are passed down from generation to generation, until, in this family; it culminated in mental instability, prostitution, and near brushes with death. But God intervened, and salvation has come to at least one household in the family, so the curse has been broken. Now, another legacy of godly behavior is being established, and instead of curses, blessings will be the inheritance of the children. Their gates are being filled with the treasures of God instead of the bitter fruits of the enemy.

There was a study done by Richard L. Dugdale in 1877 that has been used by many to show the remarkable contrast between the destinies of two families—one that lived under godly principles passed down from generation to generation, and the other that did not.

Max Jukes was an unbeliever who lived in New York. He did not accept Christian teachings or values and married a woman who believed as he did. From his marriage 1,026 descendants were studied. Of his descendants, 300 died prematurely, 100 were sent to prisons for an average of 13 years each, 190 became public prostitutes, 100 became public drunks. This family cost the state more than $6 million over the years.

On the other hand, the family of Jonathan Edwards realized a far different destiny. Jonathan Edwards was a believer, a contemporary of Max Jukes and a minister who also lived in New York. He married a woman who believed as he did, and together they passed on Christian principles and a love for God to their children. Some 729 of his descendants were studied. Of them, 300 became preachers of the gospel, 65 became college professors, 13 became presidents of universities, 60 became authors, three became U.S. congressmen, and one became vice president of the United States.

This family contributed much to our society.

It is important that parents not only teach their children, instructing them in the way of righteousness, but also know their children's friends. Proverbs 1:7-18 shows us what happens when one is enticed by ungodly friends.

The fear of the Lord is the beginning of knowledge; but fools despise wisdom and instruction. My Son, hear the instruction of thy father, and forsake not the law of thy mother: For they shall be an ornament of grace unto thy head, and chains about thy neck. My son, if sinners entice thee, consent thou not. If they say, come with us, let us lay wait for blood, let us lurk privily for the innocent without cause: Let us swallow them up alive as the grave: and whole, as those that go down into the pit...walk not thou in the way with them, restrain thy foot from their path...they lay wait for their own blood; they lurk privily for their own lives.

When our hearts turn away from God, away from the commandments He has given us; when we decide to go around the boundaries He has set up, throw off His restraints, and to do things our own way, we side with the world. The world says, "these rules are old fashioned, it's out of style, it is not for today, it's repressive, it doesn't allow me to be myself." When we begin to believe this and to act out our own will, we become deceived. The sad reality is we believe there are no consequences, even while destruction is closing in on us.

Deuteronomy 29:19-28 tells us it is foolish to believe, as so many people today seem to think, "I shall have peace, everything will be alright," even though we have turned from God and followed the dictates of our own hearts. The Word says, "as though the drunkard could be included with the sober!" As though we can escape the consequences of our actions. Although our actions may not come back to haunt us, they will come back to haunt our children, and generations to come.

If we look specifically at Deuteronomy verses 22 and 23, we can plainly see what is happening in our nation today:

> *So that the generation to come of your children that shall rise up after you, and the stranger that shall come from a far land, shall say, when they see the plagues of that land, and the sickness which the Lord hath laid upon it: And that the whole land thereof is brimstone, and salt, and burning, that it is not sown, nor beaten, nor any grass groweth therein, like the over throw of Sodom and Gomorrah, Admah, and Zeboim, which the Lord overthrew in his anger, and in his wrath.*

Our nation is suffering the plagues and sicknesses of violence, pornography, drugs, and AIDS, STD's, crime and gangs. The whole nation appears to be brimstone, salt and burning as the Word describes. Who could ever have imagined the horrible maladies affecting our society today? We are bombarded almost daily with mass murders, pornography, homosexuality, gambling, drug and alcohol addictions, children killing children—it all seems to be out of control. What has happened? In too many instances we can point to the fact that as individuals, families, and as a nation, we have turned away from God's plan. We have sown to the wind and are now reaping a whirlwind. That wind is tearing apart individual lives, families, and nations. Scripture admonishes us in Jeremiah 6:16 to:

> *...Stand ye in the ways, and see, and ask for the old paths, where is the good way, and walk therein, and ye shall find rest for your souls.*

Things have not changed much as we read the people's response to this direction from God, *"But they said, 'we will not walk in it.'"*

Elder Horace Hockett, pastor of Born Again Church in Nashville, in a message on family, stated,

"We live in a generation that is disconnected from the moral wealth of the past, is destroying all hope for the future, and lives only for the pleasures of the present. Every generation has a destiny and purpose carried forward from the generation past, to fulfill its generation's purpose and to impact the generations that follow. Psalm 33:10-12:

> *The Lord foils the plans of the nations. He thwarts the purpose of the peoples, but the plans of the Lord stand firm forever, the purposes of his heart through all generations. Blessed is the nation whose God is the Lord, the people He chose for his inheritance.*

But we have accepted for our time a curse—a generational disconnection, and we call it normal. We have been experiencing a "generation gap." *Then another generation arose that did not know the Lord! (Judges 2:10)*

It is our purpose as the children of God in this generation to receive the moral wealth of the past generations, use it to enable us to perfect our Christian walk and to finish our course. At the same time, we must equip our children (the future generation) to boldly and confidently go forward until His will is done in the earth as it is in Heaven. This is our generational purpose and destiny."

A Prayer for Our Children's Future

Rock of Ages: Jehovah

Father, thank You that the cycle of destruction that's
rooted in generational curses can be ended.
Your word teaches and admonishes us "to train up our
children in Your ways."
I confess, I have not sought Your plans for my life.
But today, I close the door to destructive habits and
unhealthy relationships.
Forgive me for allowing my heart to become hard, and
my spirit rebellious.
Forgive me, Lord, for not assuming the ultimate
responsibility of guarding the gates of my children.
Today, I yield my mind, body and will to You, as I discover
the treasures in me that have been buried in sin.
The buck stops here!
Good-bye to generational curses on my family.

Soul Ties: Partnering with Life or Death

Chapter 5

Soul Ties: Partnering with Life or Death

Relationships. They can bring us the most joy in life or they can be the cause of our deepest pain. Relationships connect us to one another, for better or for worse, in marriage, friendship, family or other associations. There are healthy and unhealthy relationships. What happens in a person's soul and spirit when a relationship moves from friendship to a sexual encounter outside of marriage? What happens when an unhealthy dependence forms between two people? At what point can intimacy become threatening to our well being?

In this chapter, "Soul Ties: Partnering with Life or Death," you will recognize situations and people caught in familiar relationship dramas. You'll also see why it's important to follow God's plan.

Before going to the next page ask the Father God to open your heart to receive divine principles that will bring you to a new level of understanding, and change your life.

> *Can a man take fire in his bosom and his*
> *clothes not be burned? Can one go upon hot*
> *coals and his feet not be burned?*
> *Proverbs 6:27, 28 (AMP)*

*But whoever commits adultery...lacks heart
and understanding (moral principal and
prudence); he who does it is destroying his
own life.*

Proverbs 6:32 (AMP)

*For [uncontrolled passion] is a fire which
consumes...[to destruction]...*

Job 31:9-12 (AMP)

Soul Ties: Partnering with Life or Death

Do not remove the ancient landmark which your fathers have set.

Proverbs 22:28 (NKJV)

Dance With Soul Ties

As a nation controlled by our own desires and lusts, we find ourselves compelled by the world's ways in our relationships. Our entire society gears us toward failure in relationships. The idea of a "boyfriend" or "girlfriend" is not according to Scripture. This concept operates on the assumption that when the 'feeling is gone' it is all right to seek another partner. Regrettably, this same mentality and behavior is taken into marriage. It is no wonder couples today have difficulty with commitment.

Dan is dating and is intimate with Monica, but can't seem to forget his last partner, Jill. Pam continues to look for her first love, Rick, in every man she dates. No one seems to last for long because they never quite measure up to Rick. She has been through ten different men trying to escape the mistakes she made with Rick.

Dan and Pam find themselves becoming more and more confused, less and less sure of who they are. This is just the tip of the iceberg called soul ties.

Dr. Dale Conaway[1] defines a soul tie as psychological, emotional, and/or physiological dependency that develops when an individual yields to a person or thing. It is the captivation of the mind, emotions, and/or will. There are two categories of soul ties: godly and ungodly. Godly soul ties are found in marriage and God-ordained friendships. When Adam and Eve became one flesh they established a godly soul tie. When Samson and Delilah committed sexual sin they developed an ungodly soul tie. Sexual sin is one way to develop a strong, ungodly soul tie that can devastate your life.

Our greatest soul tie should be to God.

> **But he that is joined unto the Lord is one spirit.**
>
> **1 Corinthians 6:17**

Being joined or cleaving to God is akin to loving God. Deuteronomy 30:20 says that we should love, obey and cleave to Him *for* He *is thy life.* The next strongest soul tie should be in the covenant of marriage. Genesis

2:24 describes the beauty of a godly soul tie in marriage: *"A man shall leave his father and mother, and shall cleave unto his wife: and they shall be one flesh."*

Adam even said that Eve was bone of his bone, and flesh of his flesh. This is literal and spiritual. In connection with godly soul ties in marriage, Dr. Conaway explains that God deliberately chose not to form Eve of the dust of the earth, but instead formed her from a part of Adam, because He wanted man and woman to share a unique intimacy. This intimacy was inclusive of the total being – spirit, soul, and body. In this, He created a physical, emotional, and spiritual bond that was to eternally unite them. It was also designed to be the basis for lifelong commitment and faithfulness to one sexual partner. We can see how godly soul ties between husband and wife can make for a stable home environment wherein to raise and nurture children. God's plan offers security, protection, and committed love to each family member.

Gary Greenwald in his book, Seductions Exposed,[2] defines a soul tie as the knitting together of two souls that can either bring tremendous blessings in a godly relationship or tremendous destruction when made with the wrong person (p. 69). Solomon describes what a blessing friendship can be when it is of God:

> *Two are better than one; because they have a good reward for their labour. For if they fall, the one will lift up his fellow: But woe to him that is alone when he falleth; for he had not another to help him up.*
> *Ecclesiastes 4:9, 10*

I

Scripture provides several examples of soul ties found in friendships or relationships that brought tremendous blessings to the people involved. We see evidence of this blessing in the relationship between Jonathan and David. The Word says the soul of Jonathan was knit with David, thus forming a soul tie. If we could form such positive bonds today what a different kind of world we would live in. Naomi and Ruth are further examples of godly soul ties. Ruth gave up everything that she had known to remain with her mother-in-law. The end result was tremendous blessing for them both. Neither of these examples expresses any compromise of God's Word. Rather, we see strength as a result of the bond that unconditional love and friendship makes.

We get in trouble when we engage in sexual and emotional relationships that compromise the Word of God.

1 Corinthians 6:16 (NKJV) explains plainly:

> *Or do you not know that he who is joined to a harlot is one body with her? For the two, he says, shall become one flesh.*

Becoming one flesh with another was within the plans of God when He made man, however, this union was reserved for the institution of marriage. Little does our promiscuous society realize that a couple engaged in sex forms a lasting bond with each other.

One young woman expressed the realization that from her freshman to her junior year as a college student she had engaged in sex with at least 65 men. She could not even remember most of their names. Her confession came as a result of hearing a teaching on soul ties where the speaker discussed several negative effects on the mind. This young lady was at a point of seeking counseling for fear that she no longer knew who she was and where she was going.

She found difficulty in focusing on schoolwork or other important matters that concerned preparing for her future after college.

Her friends tried to convince her that she was only suffering college burnout. Only in the teaching session did she come face to face with her real problem. She was on a downward spiral emotionally because she had given a piece of herself away to each of the 65 partners in the three-year period. She did not realize she was destroying her own soul by engaging in sex outside of marriage.

Her dilemma was grounded in erroneous teaching from her formative years. She was taught to protect herself from disease and unwanted pregnancies but not about the devastating effects of promiscuity. Romans 6:16 warns us:

> *Know ye not, that to whom ye yield yourselves servants to obey, his servants ye are to whom ye obey; whether of sin unto death, or of obedience unto righteousness?*

The young woman's body had become a servant to the emotions that drove her to promiscuity and the sin was slowly ebbing her very life away.

Dr. Dale Conaway writes that, "When you allow your sexuality to become perverted, your identity is never properly defined, your purpose is never fully experienced, and your God-inspired destiny will never be fully attained." The sin of fornication (sex outside of marriage) was so serious in the Old Testament that the law mandated that a man who rapes a virgin give her father money for her, marry her, and not divorce her as long as he lived. (Deuteronomy 22: 28, 29) Here we see the value placed on virginity, marriage, and responsibility.

Surrendering to illicit passions becomes expected behavior in a society that promotes unrestricted individual freedom. People find that their souls are tied to several persons. Many unsuccessful marriages result from difficulty in committing to one person. Partners usually experience affairs and/or divorce. Some people report sexual dissatisfaction or even dysfunction with the marriage partner and have mistakenly attributed it to incompatibility rather than the true spiritual root, soul ties.

When soul ties are not severed we enter into marriage with "baggage" that affects any positive relationship we attempt with our partner. "Sowing your oats" before marriage is almost a guarantee that you will experience problems within the marriage. If only we could awake to the realization that when we engage in ungodly sexual activity, we have intercourse with a human body *and* a spiritual entity. Again we are reminded in scripture of this danger:

> *But whoso committeth adultery with a woman*
> *lacketh understanding: he that doeth it*
> *destroyeth his own soul.*
>
> *Proverbs 6:32*

We open ourselves up to danger in creating ungodly soul ties grounded in the sex act and all that it encompasses. It is said that the eyes are the mirrors of the soul. This may be true when we consider how we can be drawn to a person just by the connection made with the eyes. Sometimes there seems to be a knowing that is only expressed through a look. When a man or a woman sees someone that is desirable, a connection can be made on the soulish level. It may start off with conversation. Over time the giving and exchanging of thoughts and feelings creates an increased desire to explore forbidden areas. Eventually, boundaries are crossed and touch becomes important. Holding hands, frequent touching and caressing can bring pleasure.

In one situation, a young woman was sexually attracted to a man to the point of always finding a reason to be in his presence. Through her own investigation she found where he lived. One night she showed up at his door. As she related the story, he opened the door and said nothing. He just took her by the hand, led her into the apartment and had sex with her on the floor. Sound unreal? It's a true story. He later said he knew what she wanted by the 'look in her eyes.'

As we have noted, kissing is the same as tasting another person. When sensuous kissing is introduced it becomes very symbolic of the sex act itself. There is penetration into the body of the partner through the mouth. This act can be so erotic that some people actually experience climax while kissing. This is one reason why sensuous kissing should be confined to marriage.

Any ungodly act separates us from God. When we become involved in ungodly relationships we put our desires in the place of God. If we replace Him with anything or anyone else we become guilt of idolatry. Idolatry is in complete opposition to the Word of God because it is the worship of something or someone other than God.

Codependency, another form of soul tie, can be defined as needing the persistent presence, fellowship, and nurturing of another (other than God) for personal security. This deception is usually manifested through a person's soul (mind, emotions, will) when the flesh instead of the spirit governs an individual. In its extreme form, codependency can result in the sin of fornication or homosexuality. It is idolatry. The scriptures make it plain.

And God spoke all these words, saying...thou shall have no other gods before me.

Exodus 20:1, 3

...the Lord he is God; there is none else beside him.
Deuteronomy 4:35

...and thou shalt love the Lord thy God with all thine heart, and with all thy soul, and with all thy might.
Deuteronomy 6:5

In Emotional Dependency,[3] Lori Rentzel gives the following guidelines to differentiate between the normal interdependency that happens in wholesome relationships and unhealthy dependency. Codependency is probably in operation if either party in the relationship:

- Experiences frequent jealousy or possessiveness
- Desires exclusivity
- Views other people as threats to the relationship
- Prefers to spend time alone with this friend and becomes frustrated when this doesn't happen
- Becomes irrationally angry or depressed when the other withdraws slightly

- Loses interest in other friendships
- Experiences romantic or sexual feeling leading to fantasy about the person
- Becomes preoccupied with the other person's appearance, personality and interests
- Is unwilling to make short – or long-range plans that do not include the other person
- Is unwilling to see the other's faults realistically
- Displays physical affection beyond that which is appropriate for a friendship
- Refers frequently to the other in conversation
- Feels free to speak for the other person
- Exhibits an intimacy and familiarity with this friend that causes others to feel uncomfortable or embarrassed in their presence

A healthy relationship, on the other hand, is marked by,

- Honesty
- Open communication
- Lack of jealousy
- Refusal to compromise Christian standards
- Lack of exclusivity
- Encouragement and support
- Loyalty
- Harmony
- Good rapport
- Unpretentiousness
- Transparency

In healthy relationships, we are affected by what our friends say and do, but our reactions are balanced and healthy and produce fruit of eternal life.

Pastors and other male leaders in the church can feed such co-dependent soul ties by allowing women, who sometimes live in desperation for the touch of a man, to attend to them in ways that are ungodly. Whenever the world wants to attack the church we hear horror stories of affairs and adultery in the church, many involving pastors. It is a pity to mistake carnal emotion for the anointing. Living and operating in the fleshly or soul realm is particularly dangerous for ministers. How can we try to equate God's anointing with romantic attraction? How do you think our holy God views such behavior from those who have oversight of His sheep?

> *[Israel's] watchmen are blind, they are all without knowledge; they are all dumb dogs, they cannot bark; dreaming, lying down, they love to slumber. Yes, the dogs are greedy, they can never have enough; and such are the shepherds who cannot understand; they have all turned to their own way, each one to his gain, from every quarter, one and all.*
>
> *Isaiah 56:10, 11 (AMP)*

There are stories also from pastors who tell of women who constantly come for prayer and counseling because it is the only time they receive attention from a man. Many times people come to the church because they are hurting, but when these women receive a blessing from God they mistake compassion and the gift of the anointing on the leader for a cheap, personal attraction to themselves.

Each time we enter into a sexual act we enter into covenant. Earlier we discussed gates, our senses ruled either by the Holy Spirit or our flesh. When we yield our members to sexual sin our sense gates play a major role in the making of soul ties. Amnon's rape of Tamar, discussed earlier, illustrates how the mind and flesh, when yielded to sin, can bring us to a place of debased sexual behavior.

Proverbs Chapter 7 warns of the tactics used by a harlot to seduce innocent men into her sexual trap. She appeals to the eyes by dressing in a sensual way that attracts the attention of a man. Flattery with words is her specialty so the sense of hearing is affected. In verse 13 she caught him (touch) and kissed him (taste). She appeals to his sense of smell by perfuming her bed with myrrh, aloes, and cinnamon. Finally, she entices him to have sex with her.

When our souls are not dedicated to the plan of God for our lives, we can easily be seduced by such a set up. Verse 21 says, *"With her much fair speech she caused him to yield, with the flattering of her lips she forced him."* By this time he is completely out of control and yields to his base nature. He goes to her straightway, never considering the consequences, not realizing it will cost him his life.

One woman's experience with soul ties was so pervasive that she attempted suicide twice because she could not seem to erase the memories of all the men in her life. She expressed the lack of control over her thoughts and actions. She would awaken every morning with a new resolve to change her habits, however, before the evening she was again seeking sexual release, whether through men or pornography. There are many people who walk around appearing normal and productive, however, if we could place a microscope on the inner man there would be a soul that is in torment and out of control.

In one account of soul ties the victim had become tied to more than 80 men. Without proper boundaries and affection in childhood the person developed a strong need to be touched. Now, the need to be touched is a normal one, however, unattended it can develop into a controlling monster. That was exactly the case for this victim.

Entering into sexual activity before the teen years, this woman developed an insatiable appetite for sex from anyone, even strangers, as a means to be touched. At one point the addiction was so strong that prostitution seemed the best way to get all the touching wanted. This search soon led to desolate places, living on the street and sleeping with anyone who would partake. Only the threat of a sadistic, sexual abuser brought this young victim to the realization that this lifestyle could actually mean death. If the end didn't come from violence, it could come from disease. Thank God that this young victim, who had someone to turn to for help and counseling, is now happy, delivered and dedicated to God!

There are times in our lives when we are more susceptible to soul ties than at others. Research shows that many people enter some type of soul tie at a point of vulnerability. Married people become vulnerable when the relationship with the mate is not fulfilling. Sometimes working women find themselves vulnerable when they have received a major promotion on the job or find themselves in a time of unusual stress. Believe it or not, the death of a loved one can open our gates to so much emotional pain that we become vulnerable to the seduction of our senses.

There is one instance of a young woman who

found herself very vulnerable after the death of a dear relative. She was so devastated by the separation that she felt completely alone in the world. This relative had always been there for her. To whom could she turn to replace the loss? Who else would understand her, pamper her, and affirm her as this relative had? One mistake made by this young woman was not allowing the grieving process to complete itself. The suppressed grief caused her to be much more vulnerable than she would have been ordinarily.

Just when she was at the breaking point of loneliness she found a friend who seemed to fill the void. This person was a giver, a confidante, and a consoler when memories of the past threatened to overtake her. The friend soon took over every aspect of her life. It was easy to allow the friend to take over this position. After all, she could let her friend make the major decisions and it seemed like the answer to her pain and loneliness. It wasn't long before the seemingly innocent relationship took another turn. The friend began to comfort the young woman with hugs and caresses. Soon the two were kissing and engaging in ungodly sexual activity. Unwittingly, this young woman was in a full-blown ungodly soul tie.

We are reminded in James 1:15 that when we yield to lust, it will cause us to sin. Sin, of course, will kill us if we don't find deliverance. This woman experienced such pain when trying to sever this soul tie that she would literally double over in a fetal position with pain akin to flames consuming her body. Her body ached for the touch of this person. Her life took on the dimensions of a nightmare. She even contemplated suicide. The pain was not imagined. It was real. It was so strong that death seemed the only possible escape. This woman notes that the deliverance process was as intense as the tie itself. It is painful whenever we sever or cut something away that is strongly attached.

A soul tie does not have to involve the act of sex. We can become tied to anything to which we yield our members. Many people have become tied to or even obsessed by material things such as houses, cars, money, drugs, alcohol or pornography. Anything that replaces God in our lives has the potential to become a soul tie. Soul ties can control our lives to the point of devastation if not released to God.

One story of a longtime soul tie begins with a vulnerable woman and an eager young man looking for someone to believe in. Initially, the encounter between the two was like any other that the woman had experienced over the years. She was friendly and had many acquaintances. Soon the man began to show special interest in her by way of surprise visits, compliments, and solicitation of advice. As their relationship grew, they shared more and more of their dreams and disappointments in life. They seemed to have so much in common. Over time their relationship took on a different meaning. They began to seek each other out and exclude others. Secrets and emotions were shared which began to feed a soul tie in the making. She found excuses to include him in most things that she did. He sought her out in the same way. He was very sensitive to her needs and acknowledged things about her that no one else seemed to ever notice. She became so tied to this man that he invaded her every thought. He was the last thing on her mind at night and the first thing on her mind the next morning. He was always in her dreams, which took on an element of fantasy.

Though the relationship was not a sexual one, she began to experience bouts of guilt because she felt that she was backslidden in heart. She tried rationalizing the relationship to herself, and to others who had become concerned. Her explanation was that this was a nurturing relationship and this man was just taking longer than most to realize his potential and move on. There was an excitement that both thrilled and frightened her when she realized that he was as emotionally tied to her as she was to him.

His conversations took on a more demanding tone when she did not have time to spend with him or talk on the phone. She began to sense the Spirit of God nudging her that if something were not corrected soon it would be too late. Restlessness became the torment of her life. Sleep evaded her and guilt consumed her. Relationships with others who were meaningful in her life became strained.

One day her best friend, who had been praying for her, asked if she had ever considered that the relationship with the young man might be a soul tie. It was as though her spiritual eyes came open and she faced reality for the first time in several years.

Now, realizing the problem and solving the problem are not one and the same. She tried many times to sever the tie on her own. So did the young man. Somehow it seemed that they always drifted back together again. Every series of events tied them together tighter than they had been in the beginning. She had to admit that she was no longer in control of her thoughts or desires. There were times when she prayed for God to return her to the place of fellowship with Him before she met this man. She prayed for restoration of peace of mind and a renewed desire to follow God. For some reason it was not to be. Not until she repented of her idolatry did God begin to move in her life and deliver her from the devastating effects of the soul tie.

It is so important that we seek complete deliverance from soul ties because if the emotion is only suppressed, it will rear its ugly head at the most inopportune time. One testimony deals with a couple that had an unsuccessful relationship. The relationship had been over for several years. One of the partners considered themselves completely delivered from the pain and emotions of the breakup until the other person re-entered her presence. Even though there was no longer any desire for a relationship, still she felt involuntarily drawn to the person. There were times when jealousy ruled. Other times there was elation at the slightest bit of attention paid by the former partner. Although outwardly there was an appearance of nonchalance, inwardly there was emotional turmoil.

The unusual part of this story is that although the person did not truly want to rekindle the relationship, there was difficulty in thinking that the former partner would prefer someone else to her. Eventually the turmoil built to a point that a resolution was crucial. Some unacceptable solutions included running away, attempting to restart the relationship, or romancing a dead dream. The only acceptable solutions were fasting and prayer for complete deliverance. God is true to his Word. Complete deliverance came. The emotional turmoil that once gripped was no longer present.

Scores of stories and accounts could be discussed here, however, you may ask at this point, is there a balm in Gilead? Is there any hope? Can I be delivered? The good news is that God's Word is powerful, and He is able and willing to deliver from the power of destructive soul ties. There may be as many approaches to deliverance as there are people and personalities; however, one thing is required before the deliverance process can begin. It is imperative that we turn to God. We must remember that *nothing* is impossible with God (Mark 9:23). We have hope for complete recovery but it is important to note that *there is no magic solution*. There are some steps that you must be willing to take to be healed and reach your God-given purpose.

Robert Burney in his book <u>The Dance of Wounded Souls</u> [4] discusses how some people can go to counseling for 20 years and still operate in the same behaviors. All too often we treat symptoms (behavior) and not the root causes (dysfunctional souls). The knowledge is there but the application seems to be missing. Too many of us are looking for a *quick fix* or someone to blame. Robert Burney again offers excellent advice when he says our perspective must change. In fact, Burney believes that perspective is the key to recovery from codependency. It is also necessary to recover from soul ties.

According to Burney, "when we enlarge our perspective, the closer we get to the cause instead of just dealing with the symptoms." Our perspective of God, self and others determines our relationship *to* God, self, and others. There can be no growth until we redirect our perspective. When we submit to God He can cause us to operate from the spirit man, which is having "the eyes to see, and the ears to hear – and the ability to feel the emotional energy that is Truth." The enemy would have us believe a lie and be damned. (2 Thessalonians 2:11, 12)

Before full recovery can take place it is necessary that we face the truth of our condition. No more suppression of emotions but a realistic look at what we feel and why. Then we must proceed to confessing, repenting of, and forsaking the soul tie. Confessing and renouncing soul ties is essential for deliverance. Proverbs 28:13 says, "*He that covereth his sins shall not prosper: but whoso confesseth and forsaketh them shall have mercy.* We must come into agreement with God's view of sin and renounce it. Forsaking means to leave behind, release, let go, cut off, neglect. We must be willing to stop engaging in ungodly activities that promote soul ties.

That means guarding our gates, and bringing our soul (minds, emotions and wills) into subjection to our spirit and the Word of God. Romans 10:10 says, *"For with the heart man believeth unto righteousness; and with the mouth confession is made unto salvation."*

As we ask for God's help to change, we can expect deliverance. For some it may be instant and easier than we ever imagined. For others it may be a longer process, not because it takes God that long, but because it may take us longer to change our perspectives and catch hold to faith. God has promised us healing and made it available through His Son, Jesus Christ.

> ***Surely he hath borne our griefs, and carried our sorrows...but he was wounded for our transgressions, he was bruised for our iniquities: the chastisement of our peace was upon him; and with his stripes we are healed.***
> ***Isaiah 53:4, 5***

God is waiting and willing to restore us to wholeness if we will surrender our will to Him. Deliverance may involve counseling, meditating the Word, prayer and fasting or accountability. In one soul tie session the Lord directed the teacher to lead those who professed they had soul ties and wanted deliverance, to pray a repentant prayer. After the prayer the Holy Spirit said to write the names of those with whom they had ungodly soul ties. These names were placed in a metal container and burned. The burning was symbolic of destroying the tie just as baptizing in water is symbolic of being buried and resurrected with Jesus.

Those who have for many years counseled and encouraged people tell thousands of stories that could have been shared here. We pray that their experiences will help you come to a place in your relationships with others and with God that brings complete wholeness.

> *Praise the Lord, all you nations; extol him, all you peoples. For great is his love toward us, and the faithfulness of the Lord endures forever. Praise the Lord.*
>
> **Psalm 117**

1. Dr. Dale Conaway, "Sex is a Spiritual Act." *Reprint authorized by publisher's agent.*

2. Taken from "Seductions Exposed" by Gary Greenwald. *Used by permission of the publisher, Whitaker House, New Kensington, PA*

3. Taken from "Emotional Dependency" by Lori Rentzel. *(c) 1984, 1987, 1990 Lori Thorkelson Rentzel. Used by permission of InterVarsity Press, P.O. Box 1400, Downers Grove, IL 60515. www.ivpress.com*

4. Codependence: The Dance of Wounded Souls by Robert Burney, *copyright 1995, Joy to You & Me Enterprises. Reprinted by permission of Robert Burney and Joy to You & Me, P.O. Box 977 Canbria, CA 93428. www.Joy2MeU.com*

A Prayer for Godly Relationships

Jehovah Nakah

The Lord Will Guide Thee

Forgive and deliver me, Lord God, from the spirit
of lust and the addiction of sexual sin.
Teach me through godly principles how to form
wholesome and healthy relationships by exercising
discipline while staying within spiritual boundaries.
Teach me to discern unhealthy ties
that begin the process of destruction.
Thank You for opening my eyes to see that no human
being can love and fulfill me like You can.
You are El Shaddai, more than enough. Forgive me for
looking to humans to fill my emptiness, when You are the
Creator who knows just how to touch me in the right way.
Today, I choose to only enter into healthy soul ties.
Thank You for Your Word that promises to meet my every
need: physically, emotionally, and spiritually.
Thank You for keeping me pure, whole, and unsoiled so
that I may reflect You.

A Tribute

To Our Dear Sister, Gloria Dennis:

Thank you for providing encouragement and sustenance [both physical and emotional] during the writing of this book. Your faithfulness has already paved the way for your destiny.

With Love,

Your Covenant Sisters
Orlando, Florida - 2000

God's Faithfulness

Great is thy faithfulness, in the spring of my life. When my spirit knows no bounds and laughter comes so easily. When a song breaks forth from my heart for no apparent reason and time seems endless.

Great is thy faithfulness, in the summer of my life. When dreams of greatness are invoked and new horizons are my goals. Boundless love for life overflows into my relationships, causing me to enjoy the ordinary pleasures and pastimes of life.

Great is thy faithfulness, in the autumn of my life. When patience manifests herself as a value, and attachments no longer weigh me down. The voice of the Spirit calls me to the ancient paths, to a life of sacrifice.

Great is thy faithfulness in the unity of my life. When higher motives motivate me to outgrow less mature and satisfying pleasures. I see the sacredness in all things and every moment as a gift.

I follow the light of truth to my destiny.
Great is Thy faithfulness

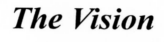

The Vision

Vision of Fashioned In His Image, Inc.

Founded in 1982 by Kiwanis Hockett, Associate Pastor of Born Again Church in Nashville, TN, Fashioned In His Image was birthed out a need to touch the lives of women on a natural as well as spiritual level. "When we started, many women from the neighborhood were drawn to the church," Sister Hockett remembered. "They were getting saved, but they still had broken hearts and bruised bodies and souls."

There were so many needs: marital problems, mental and physical abuse, and emotional wounds. Women, within the church and outside, were struggling with these and other issues every day. "As I prayed for direction," Sister Hockett continued, "I felt strongly that we needed to provide more support and help for the ladies. I knew they needed a strong scriptural foundation to know they could be overcomers, but they also needed to be ministered to naturally."

The Lord gave her two biblical passages that have become the scriptural basis for the women's fellowship: Romans 12:1-2: *"I beseech you therefore brethren, by the mercies of God, that ye present your bodies a living sacrifice, holy, acceptable unto God, which is your reasonable service. And be not conformed to this world: but be ye transformed by the renewing of your mind, that ye may prove what is that good, and acceptable, and perfect, will of God"*...and Philippians 3:21: *"Who shall change our vile body, that it may be fashioned like unto his glorious body, according to the working whereby he is able even to subdue all things unto himself."*

FIHI's mission is to help women grow into the image and likeness of Christ, and into the fullness of what God intended for womanhood through teaching, counseling, evangelizing, and networking.

Evangelism and community outreach projects are an important focus, and many other ministries have been birthed out of Fashioned In His Image to serve women. They include: My Sister's Keeper, a mentoring program for young women ages 13-30 which meets weekly to discuss challenging issues such as sex, self-esteem, substance and other abuse, and family crisis; Teen Save, a suicide awareness program; Sisters In The Word, a women's Bible study that meets monthly each fall and winter in homes and on college campuses throughout the city and surrounding areas; Camp CeCe, which provides an outstanding experience in Christian day camping, promoting adventure, inspiration, character building, creativity, and confidence; Foundations, a program serving as a multi-purpose resource to teenage mothers; Quiet Hands/Designing Hearts, which encourages the development of hand-craft skills; The Total You, designed to enhance personal leadership development and personal style; and an International Annual Women of Destiny Conference.

"God is continually blessing us as women in so many ways, but we can't keep these blessings to ourselves," says Sister Hockett. "We were created to be a blessing...to our families, our church, and the world."

I'm A Part of the Fellowship of The Unashamed

The die has been cast, the decision has been made,
Stepped over the line.
I won't look back, let up, slow down, or back away.

My past is redeemed, my present makes sense,
And my future is secure.
I'm finished and done with low living, sight walking,
small planning,
Smooth knees, colorless dreams, tamed visions,
mundane talking,
Cheap giving and dwarted goals.
I no longer need preeminence, prosperity, position,
Promotion, plaudits, or popularity.
I don't have to be right, first, tops, recognized,
Praised, regarded, or rewarded.
I now live by faith,
I lean on His presence and walk with patience.

I live by prayer and labor with power.
My face is set, my gait is fast,
My goal is known, my road is narrow,
And the way is rough.

My companions are few,
My guide is reliable,
And my mission is clear.

I cannot be bought, compromised, detoured, lured away,
Turned back, diluted or delayed.
I will not flinch in the face of sacrifice.
I will not hesitate in the presence of the adversary,
I will not negotiate at the table of the enemy
Or ponder at the pool of popularity.
I will not meander in the maze of mediocrity.
I won't give up, shut up, let up,
Until I have stayed up, stood up, prayed up, paid up,
And spoke up for the cause of Christ.

I am a disciple of Christ.
I must go till He comes, give till I drop,
Preach till all know, and work until He comes.
And when He comes for His own,
He will have no problem recognizing me.
My banners will be clear.

I am a part of the fellowship of the unashamed.

Anonymous

The Writing Group

The writing group:

Kiwanis Hockett is the wife of Pastor Horace Hockett of Born Again Church, Nashville, Tennessee. She is the associate pastor and is truly an anointed woman of God. Sister Kitty, as she is affectionately known, serves the ministry in various leadership capacities, but her heart is to minister to women. She founded Fashioned In His Image, Inc. out of her desire to meet the needs of women within and outside the ministry. She and her husband have two sons.

Dr. Sandra Holt is director of the Honors Program at Tennessee State University in Nashville, Tennessee, where she also is associate professor of Communications. A gifted teacher, motivational speaker, and consultant she is widely sought out for conferences and seminars for industry, government, and academia. Dr. Holt is married to Elijah Holt and is the mother of four and grandmother to five.

Lilly Lester is an advocate for children. Now retired, she served as an administrator in early childhood education for more than 20 years. Lilly is a published author and poet, and a member of the International Society of Poets. She is an anointed teacher and speaker. Her hobbies are writing, reading, and traveling. She is married to George Lester, the mother of two children, and the grandmother of three.

Catina Marshall is founder of Foundations, a non-profit program under Fashioned In His Image, Inc. that is committed to building the self-esteem and parenting skills of young unwed mothers. Catina is a gifted teacher and administrator. She enjoys reading and racquetball. Catina is married to Jackie Marshall. She and her husband have three children and one grandchild.

Dannell Meddling is an ordained minister, writer, and anointed teacher with a passion and calling to intercession. She also is gifted in administration, which is her vocation. Dannell is a motivator and exhorter and uses her gifting to propel women to reach their fullest potential and purpose in Christ.

Jacqueline Wilson is an ordained minister and Communications Director for Born Again Church in Nashville, Tennessee, where she also serves on the Pastoral Council and as Director of the Ministers in Training Program. A graduate of RHEMA Bible Training Center in Broken Arrow, Oklahoma; she is a former writer for *The Word of Faith Magazine* of Kenneth Hagin Ministries.

Debra Winans is a teacher, writer, sought after conference speaker, and CEO of Image and Leadership Development, a consulting firm she founded. Her mission is to see the church move from average to Excellence! Debra is anointed to serve others. She is the mother of two children.

<u>To Order</u>

Please send $10.95 plus $3.00 Shipping & Handling:

Make all checks/money orders payable to:

Fashioned In His Image, Inc.
P.O. Box 281874
Nashville, TN 37228

To contact the authors go to www.fihi.net

****

*Study Guide will be available soon......

Printed in the United States
18561LVS00001B/331-453